Salman Rushdie's
Haroun and the Sea of Stories

SALMAN RUSHDIE'S

Haroun and the Sea of Stories

adapted by
Tim Supple and David Tushingham

faber and faber

First published in 1998
by Faber and Faber Limited
3 Queen Square London WC1N 3AU

Typeset by Faber and Faber Ltd
Printed in England by Mackays of Chatham plc, Chatham, Kent

A CIP record for this book
is available from the British Library

ISBN 0–571–19693–4

2 4 6 8 10 9 7 5 3 1

Characters

This stage version of **Haroun and the Sea of Stories** has been conceived for twelve performers to work as a chorus, each of whom is involved in telling the story at all times. How they do this may change from scene to scene – or even within scenes. Everyone has one or a series of characters to represent. In addition they also sing and contribute to the show musically. But the performers also narrate the story and, where appropriate, represent certain aspects of it physically. So, in addition to the credited parts, they also play inhabitants of the sad city, passengers on the bus to K, Guppees, Chupwalas, etc.

In the original production, which premièred at the Royal National Theatre, London, on 25 September 1998, the parts were combined as follows:

Haroun Khalifa Nitin Chandra Ganatra
Rashid Khalifa Nabil Shaban
Soraya Khalifa/Goopy Sapna Hindocha
Mr Sengupta/Khattam-Shud/The Walrus Sam Dastor
Oneeta Sengupta/Bagha/Princess Batcheat Sudha Bhuchar
Unsmiling Man in G/Swan Boat/Mudra, the Shadow Warrior/Passer-By Dhobi Oparei
Unsmiling Man in G/Mali/Mudra's Shadow/Chupwala Ambassador/An Egghead Robert Bowman
Mr Butt, the Bus Driver/Butt the Hoopoe Stephen Finegold
Second Bus Driver/Iff, the Water Genie/Passer-By Nizwar Karanj
Snooty Buttoo/General Kitab Simon Nagra

Snooty Buttoo's soldier/Peacock Bed/Prince Bolo Paul Bazely
Snooty Buttoo's soldier/Turtle Bed/Princess in rescue story/Blabbermouth Syreeta Kumar

Musicians
Ansuman Biswas (tabla, dhol, gongs, percussion, santoor, ramsingha, computer-generated treatments)
Adrian Lee ('ud, mandola, dobro, siter, keyboards, dhol, percussion)
N. Tiken Singh (saranta, pena, bansuri, ramsingha, harmonium, dhol, dholak, Metei pung, congo-set, langde, percussion)
Singer Sapna Hindocha

Director Tim Supple
Designer and co-deviser Melly Still
Lighting Designer Paule Constable
Music Adrian Lee
Artistic Associate David Tushingham
Sound Designer Christopher Shutt
Magic Consultant Paul Kieve
Juggling Consultant The Gandini Juggling Project
Dance Instructor N. Tiken Singh

1. THE TERRIBLE QUESTION

Chorus There was once, in the country of Alifbay, a sad city, the saddest of cities, a city so ruinously sad that it had forgotten its name.

Chorus In the north of the sad city stood mighty factories in which (so I'm told) sadness was actually manufactured, packaged and sent all over the world, which never seemed to get enough of it.

Chorus Black smoke poured out of the chimneys of the sadness factories and hung over the city like bad news.

Chorus And in the depths of the city, beyond an old zone of ruined buildings that looked like broken hearts, there lived a happy young fellow by the name of Haroun, the only child of the storyteller Rashid Khalifa, whose cheerfulness was famous throughout that unhappy metropolis, and whose never-ending stream of tall, short and winding tales had earned him not one but two nicknames.

Chorus To his admirers Rashid was the Ocean of Notions but to his jealous rivals he was the Shah of Blah.

Chorus To his wife, Soraya, Rashid was for many years as loving a husband as anyone could wish for, and during these years Haroun grew up in a home in which, instead of misery and frowns, he had his father's ready laughter and his mother's sweet voice raised in song.

Chorus Then something went wrong. Soraya stopped singing, in the middle of a line, as if someone had thrown a switch.

Soraya Rashid Khalifa was so busy making up and telling stories he didn't notice.

Chorus But then Rashid was a busy man, in constant

demand, he was the Ocean of Notions, the famous Shah of Blah.

Haroun Haroun often thought of his father as a juggler, because his stories were really lots of different tales juggled together, and Rashid kept them going in a sort of dizzy whirl, and never made a mistake.
Where do all these stories come from?

Rashid From the great Story Sea. Glug glug glug. I drink the Story Waters and then I feel full of steam.

Haroun Where do you keep this hot water?

Rashid It comes out of an invisible tap installed by one of the Water Genies.

Haroun I've never seen a Water Genie.

Rashid You're never up in time to see the milkman, but you don't mind drinking the milk. You have to be a subscriber.

Haroun And how do you become a subscriber?

Rashid Oh, that's much Too Complicated To Explain. Now kindly desist from this Iffing and Butting and be happy with the stories you enjoy.

Soraya joins Haroun and Rashid.

Haroun Why don't you have any more children?

Rashid We used up our full quota of child-stuff just in making you. It's all packed in there, enough for maybe four–five kiddies. Yes, sir, there's more to you than the blinking eye can see.

Soraya We tried. This child business is not an easy thing. Think of the poor Senguptas.

Haroun The Senguptas lived upstairs.

2

Chorus Mr Sengupta was a clerk at the offices of the City Corporation and he was as sticky-thin and whiny-voiced and mingy as his wife Oneeta was generous and loud and wobbly-fat.

Chorus They had no children at all, and as a result Oneeta Sengupta paid more attention to Haroun than he really cared for.

Chorus Mr Sengupta ignored Haroun, but was always talking to Soraya.

Sengupta That husband of yours, excuse me if I mention, he's got his head stuck in the air and his feet off the ground. What are all these stories? Life is not a storybook or joke shop. All this fun will come to no good. What's the use of stories that aren't even true?

Haroun What's the use of stories that aren't even true?

Chorus Haroun couldn't get the terrible question out of his head.

2. THE BROKEN CLOCKS

Chorus On the day that everything went wrong, Haroun was on his way home from school when he was caught in the first downpour of the rainy season.

Chorus Miss Oneeta was standing on her upstairs balcony, shaking like a jelly; and if it hadn't been raining, Haroun might have noticed that she was crying.

Chorus He went indoors and found Rashid the storyteller looking as if he'd stuck his face out of the window, because his eyes and cheeks were soaking wet, even though his clothes were dry.

Chorus Haroun's mother, Soraya, had run off with Mr Sengupta.

Chorus At eleven a.m. precisely, she had sent Rashid into Haroun's room to search for some missing socks.

Chorus Rashid heard the front door slam, and, an instant later, the sound of a car in the lane.

Chorus He returned to the living room to find his wife gone and a taxi speeding round the corner.

Chorus The clock still stood at eleven o'clock exactly.

Chorus Rashid picked up a hammer and smashed every clock in the house, including the one on Haroun's bedside table.

Haroun What did you have to break my clock for?

Chorus From this moment Haroun found he couldn't keep his mind on anything for very long or, to be precise, for more than eleven minutes at a time.

Oneeta Eleven o'clock when his mother exited. Now

4

comes this problem of eleven minutes. Cause is located in his pussy-collar-jee. Owing to pussy-collar-jeecal sadness, the young master is stuck fast on his eleven number and cannot get to twelve.

Haroun That's not true.

Chorus Soraya had left a note.

The note is passed round and read aloud.

Rashid You are only interested in pleasure, but a proper man would know that life is a serious business.

Sengupta Your brain is full of make-believe, so there is no room in it for facts.

Soraya Mr Sengupta has no imagination at all. This is OK by me.

Haroun Tell Haroun I love him, but I can't help it, I have to do this now.

Note ends.

Rashid What to do, son? Storytelling is the only work I know.

Haroun (*loses his temper*) What's the point of it? What's the point of stories that aren't even true?

Chorus Haroun wanted to get those words back, to pull them out of his father's ears and shove them back into his own mouth; but of course he couldn't.

Chorus And that was why he blamed himself soon afterwards when an Unthinkable Thing happened.

3 . THE ARKS

Chorus It was almost election time. And it was well known that nobody ever believed anything a politico said.

Chorus But everyone had complete faith in Rashid because he always admitted everything he told them was completely untrue. So the politicos needed Rashid to help them win the people's votes.

Chorus Some days later Rashid Khalifa was invited to perform by politicos from the Town of G and the nearby Valley of K, which nestled in the Mountains of M.

Rashid We should go. In the Town of G and the Valley of K the weather is still fine, whereas here the air is too weepy for words.

Oneeta Tip-top plan. Yes, both of you, go. It will be like a little holiday, and no need to worry about me sitting sitting all by myself.

Chorus They were met at the Railway Station in the Town of G by two unsmiling men.

Haroun They look like villains to me.

Chorus The two men drove Rashid and Haroun straight to the political rally.

Chorus And arrived at a thick forest of human beings.

Chorus A crowd of people sprouting in all directions like leaves on jungle trees.

Chorus Then the unthinkable thing happened.

Chorus Rashid went out on stage in front of that vast crowd.

Chorus Haroun watched him from the wings.

Chorus The poor storyteller opened his mouth, and . . .

Rashid Ark.

Chorus Found it was as empty as his heart.

Rashid Ark, ark, ark.

Chorus The Shah of Blah sounded like a stupid crow.

Man 1 The two men accused Rashid of having taken a bribe from their rivals.

Man 2 And suggested that they might cut off his tongue and other items also.

Rashid And Rashid, close to tears, kept repeating that he couldn't understand why he had dried up, and promising to make it up to them.
In the Valley of K I will be terrifico, magnifique.

Man 1 Better you are, or else out comes that tongue from your lying throat.

Haroun So when does the plane leave for K?

Man 2 Plane? Plane? His papa's stories won't take off but the brat wants to fly! No plane for you, master and sonny. Catch a blasted bus.

4. THE BUS STATION

Haroun Haroun followed Rashid across a dusty court-yard with walls covered in strange warnings:

Chorus
  IF YOU TRY TO RUSH OR ZOOM
  YOU ARE SURE TO MEET YOUR DOOM

Chorus
  ALL THE DANGEROUS OVERTAKERS
  END UP SAFE AT UNDERTAKERS

Chorus
  LOOK OUT! SLOW DOWN! DON'T BE FUNNY!
  LIFE IS PRECIOUS! CARS COST MONEY!

Rashid Rashid went to buy a ticket.

Small dust-clouds rush back and forth like little desert whirlwinds. These clouds are full of human beings carrying a mind-boggling array of luggage and other possessions.

One driver starts his engine and behaves as if he is about to leave. At once a bunch of passengers rushes towards him. Then he switches off his engine with an innocent smile, while on the far side of the courtyard a different bus starts up and the passengers start running all over again.

This continues until two separate dust-clouds of scurrying passengers collide in an explosion of all their multifarious possessions.

Haroun, without meaning to, begins to laugh.

Mr Butt You're a tip-top type. You see the funny side. An accident is truly a sad and cruel thing, but but but – crash! Wham! Spatoosh! How it makes one giggle and hoot.

At your service, my goodname is Butt, driver of the Number One Super Express Mail Coach to the Valley of K.

Haroun And my goodname is Haroun. If you mean what you say about being of service, there is something you can do.

Mr Butt It was a figure of speech. But but but I will stand by it! A figure of speech is a shifty thing: it can be twisted or it can be straight. But Butt's a straight man, not a twister. What's your wish, my young mister?

Haroun Rashid had often told Haroun about the beauty of the road from the Town of G to the Valley of K, a road that climbed like a serpent through the Pass of H toward the Tunnel of I (which was also known as J).

Mr Butt When the road emerged from the Tunnel, the traveller saw before him the Valley of K with its golden fields and silver mountains and with the Dull Lake at its heart – a view spread out like a magic carpet, waiting for someone to take a ride.

Haroun No man can be sad who looks upon that sight, Rashid had said.
Front-row seats in the Mail Coach all the way to the Dull Lake, passing through the Tunnel of I (also known as J) before sunset.

Mr Butt But but but, the hour is already late.

Haroun Otherwise the whole point will be lost.

Mr Butt But but but so what? The beautiful view! To cheer up the sad dad. No problem!

The bus forms and all the other passengers get on board.

Rashid So when Rashid staggered out of the ticket office he found Haroun waiting on the steps of the Mail Coach with the best seats reserved inside, and the motor running.

As I may have mentioned, young Haroun Khalifa: more to you than meets the blinking eye.

Mr Butt Yahoo! Varoom!

The coach rockets off, narrowly missing another sign:

Chorus
IF FROM SPEED YOU GET YOUR THRILL
TAKE PRECAUTION – MAKE YOUR WILL

It travels faster and faster. The passengers hoot and howl with excitement and fear.

Haroun Don't we need to stop for the letters?

Rashid Do we need to go so blinking fast?

Mr Butt Need to stop? Need to go so quickly? Well, Need's a slippery snake, that's what it is. The boy here says that you, sir, Need A View Before Sunset, and maybe it's so and maybe no. And some might say that the boy here Needs A Mother, and maybe it's so and maybe no. And it's been said of me that Butt Needs Speed, but but but it may be that my heart truly needs a Different Sort Of Thrill. Oh, Need's a funny fish: it makes people untruthful.
  Hurrah! The snow line! Icy patches ahead! Crumbling road surface! Hairpin bends! Danger of avalanches! Full speed ahead!

The Mail Coach rushes up into the Mountains of M, swinging around terrifying curves with a great squealing of tyres. The luggage begins to shift about in a worrying way.

Mr Butt Here, two weeks ago, occurred a major disaster. Bus plunged into gully, all persons killed, sixty–seventy lives minimum. God! Too sad! If you desire I can stop for taking of photographs.

Passengers Yes, stop, stop.

But Mr Butt goes even faster instead.

Mr Butt Too late. Already it is far behind. Requests must be made more promptly if I am to comply.

Roadside notices warn of extra danger in words so severe they no longer rhyme.

Chorus
DRIVE LIKE HELL AND YOU WILL GET THERE.

Chorus
BE DEAD SLOW OR BE DEAD.

Everyone falls into a scared and frozen silence.

Haroun Any moment now I am going to be wiped out, like a word on a blackboard, one swoosh of the duster and I'll be gone for good.

Suddenly everything goes dark. Noise returns: screams, the skidding of tyres.

This is it!

And then they are in a place with smooth walls curving up around them, and rows of yellow lights set in the ceiling above.

Mr Butt Tunnel, One View coming up. Like I said: no problem.
They came out of the Tunnel of I, and Mr Butt stopped the coach so that everyone could enjoy the sight of the sun setting over the Valley of K, with its fields of gold . . .

Haroun Which were really saffron . . .

Mr Butt And its silver mountains . . .

Haroun Which were really covered in glistening, pure white snow . . .

Mr Butt And its Dull Lake . . .

Haroun Which didn't look dull at all.

Rashid Thanks, son. For some time I thought we were all done for, finito, khattam-shud.

Haroun Khattam-Shud. Wasn't that a story . . .?

Rashid Khattam-Shud is the Arch-Enemy of all Stories, even of Language itself. He is the Prince of Silence and the Foe of Speech. And because everything ends, because dreams end, stories end, life ends, at the finish of everything we use his name. 'It's finished,' we tell each other, 'it's over. Khattam-Shud: The End.'

Haroun This place is doing you good. Your crazy stories are starting to come back.

6. THE DULL LAKE

Chorus It was dark when the coach arrived at the bus depot in K.

The bus stops and the passengers, including Rashid and Haroun, get off. We see Snooty Buttoo, escorted by two armed soldiers.

Chorus They were greeted by the Boss himself, the Top Man in the ruling party of the Valley, the Candidate in the forthcoming elections, on whose behalf Rashid had agreed to appear.

Buttoo Esteemed Mr Rashid. An honour for us. A legend comes to town. The name is Buttoo.

Haroun Almost the same as the Mail Coach driver!

Buttoo Not at all the same as any bus driver. Suffering Moses! Do you know to whom you speak? Do I look the bus driver type?
Respected Mr Rashid to the lakeside.

Haroun Waiting for them was a boat in the shape of a swan.

This appears and they get in.

Buttoo Nothing but the best for distinguished Mr Rashid. Tonight you stay in the finest houseboat on the Lake, as my guest. I trust it will not prove too humble for a grandee as exalted as you.

Haroun He sounded polite, but he was really being insulting. Why did Rashid put up with it?

The Swan Boat sets off across the lake.

Chorus Haroun looked down into the water of the Dull Lake.

Haroun It seemed to be full of strange currents, criss-crossing in intricate patterns.

Chorus Then the swan-boat passed what looked like a carpet floating on the water's surface.

Rashid Floating garden. You weave lotus roots together to make a carpet then you can grow vegetables right here on the lake.

Haroun Don't be sad.

Buttoo Sad? Unhappy? Surely eminent Mr Rashid is not dissatisfied with the arrangements?

Rashid Sir, not so. This is an affair of the heart.

Buttoo Not to worry, unique Mr Rashid. She may have left you but there are plenty more fish in the sea.

Rashid Ah, but you must go a long, long way to find an Angel Fish.

Chorus As if in response to Rashid's words, the weather changed and a mist rushed at them across the water.

Haroun Haroun had already smelled unhappiness on the night air, and this sudden mist positively stank of unhappiness and gloom.

Buttoo Phoo! Who made that smell? Come on, admit.

Haroun It's the mist. It's a Mist of Misery.

Buttoo Lenient Mr Rashid, it seems the boy wants to cover up his stink-making with inventions. I fear he is too much like the folk of this foolish Valley – crazy for make-believe. For this reason, I have turned, eloquent Mr Rashid, to you. You will tell happy stories, and the people will believe you, and be happy, and vote for me.

A harsh, hot wind blows across the Lake. It burns into

their faces, and the water becomes choppy and wild.

Haroun It's not in the least Dull, this Lake. It's positively temperamental! This must be the Moody Land!

It made sense: Rashid was sad, so the Mist of Misery enveloped the swan-boat; and Snooty Buttoo was so full of hot air, it wasn't surprising he'd conjured up this boiling wind.

Rashid The Moody Land was only a story, Haroun. Here we're somewhere real. (*To Buttoo*) Surely you don't want me to tell just sugar-and-spice tales? People can delight in the saddest stuff, as long as they find it beautiful.

Buttoo Nonsense, nonsense! Terms of your engagement are crystal clear! If you want pay, then just be gay!

The hot wind begins to blow with redoubled force. The oarsmen cry out in panic. Snooty Buttoo seems to take the weather conditions as a personal insult and shrieks infuriatedly.

Haroun OK. Everybody listen. This is very important: everybody just stop talking. Not a word. On the count of three, one two three.

At once the boiling breeze falls away, the thunder and lightning stops. The smelly mist, however, remains.

(*To Rashid*) Just do one thing for me. Think of the happiest times you can remember. Think of the view of the Valley of K we saw when we came through the Tunnel of I. Think of your wedding day. Please.

A few moments later the mist tears apart and drifts away on a cool breeze.

You see, it wasn't only a story after all.

Rashid You're a blinking good man in a tight spot, Haroun Khalifa. Hats off to you.

Haroun The houseboat was called Arabian Nights Plus One.

Buttoo Because even in all the Arabian Nights you will never have a night like this.

The boat's windows have each been cut in the shape of a fabulous bird, fish or beast. They go inside.

Haroun The walls were lined with shelves full of leather-bound volumes.

Rashid But most of these turned out to be fakes.

Haroun One shelf, however, bore a set of real books in a language Haroun could not read, and illustrated with the strangest pictures he had ever seen.

Buttoo Erudite Mr Rashid, you in your line of work will be interested in these. Here for your delectation and edification is the entire collection of tales known as the Ocean of the Streams of Story. If you ever run out of material you will find plenty in here.

Rashid Run out! What are you saying?

Buttoo Touchy Mr Rashid! Of course we await your recital with full confidence.

Rashid In the exact centre of Rashid's room stood an enormous painted peacock. The boatmen removed its back to reveal a large and comfortable bed.

One of the soldiers turns into the peacock bed.

Haroun Haroun had the adjoining room, in which he found an equally outsize turtle, which likewise became a bed when the boatmen removed its shell.

The other soldier now becomes the turtle bed.

Thank you, it is very pleasant.

Buttoo Very pleasant? Inappropriate young person, you are aboard Arabian Nights Plus One! Very pleasant does not cover it at all! Admit, at the very least, that it is all Super-Marvelloso, Incredibable, and wholly Fantastick!

Rashid It is, as Haroun has stated, very pleasant indeed. Now we will sleep. Goodnight.

Buttoo Tomorrow, unappreciative Mr Rashid, it is your turn. Let us see how 'very pleasant' your audience finds you.

Haroun finds it difficult to get to sleep. He is disturbed by noises from Rashid's room next door and goes to investigate.

Rashid It's no use – I'm finished, finished for good! I'll get up on stage and find nothing in my mouth but arks. Then they'll slice me in pieces, finito, khattam-shud! Better stop fooling myself, go into retirement, cancel my subscription – because the magic's gone, ever since she left.
  Who's there?

Haroun It's me. Couldn't sleep. I think it's the turtle. It's just too weird.

Rashid I've been having trouble with this peacock myself. For me a turtle would be better. How do you feel about the bird?

Haroun OK.

Haroun and Rashid exchange bedrooms.

8. IFF, THE WATER GENIE

*Iff, the Water Genie, enters Rashid's room, where Haroun
is now sleeping. Haroun is again woken by noises and
looks to see where they are coming from. Iff is initially
too busy to notice him.*

Iff Put it in, take it out. The fellow comes up here, so I
have to come and install it, rush job, never mind my
workload. Then wham, bam, he cancels his subscription,
and guess who has to come back and take the equipment
out, right away, pronto, you'd think there was a fire. Now
where did I put the blasted thing? Where's it gone?

> *The floorboard on which Haroun is standing creaks. Iff
> sees Haroun, whirls around in surprise and drops what
> looks like a monkey wrench. Haroun is the first to pick
> it up and will not let go.*

Enough's enough, party's over. Give it back.

Haroun No.

Iff The Disconnector. Hand it over, return to sender,
restore to rightful owner.

Haroun Now Haroun noticed that the tool he held was
more fluid than solid, made up of thousands of little
veins, all held together by some unbelievable, invisible
force.

You're not getting it back till you tell me what you're
doing here. Are you a burglar?

Iff Mission impossible to divulge, top secret, classified,
eyes-only info; certainly not to be revealed to smartypants
boys who snatch what isn't theirs and then accuse other
people of being thieves.

Haroun I'll wake my father.

Iff No. No adults. I knew this would be a terrible day.

Haroun I'm waiting.

Iff I am the Water Genie, Iff, from the Ocean of the Streams of Story.

Haroun You're really one of those Genies my father told me about?

Iff Supplier of Story Water from the Great Story Sea. However, I regret to report, the gentleman no longer requires the service; has discontinued narrative activities, packed it in. He has cancelled his subscription. Hence my presence, for purposes of Disconnection. To which end, please to return my Tool.

Haroun How did he send the message? I've been with him all the time.

Iff By the usual means. A P2C2E.

Haroun What's that?

Iff A Process Too Complicated To Explain.

Haroun You've made a mistake. My father has not given up. You can't cut off his Story Water.

Iff Orders. All queries to be taken up with the Grand Comptroller, P2C2E House, Gup City, Kahani. The Walrus.

Haroun The Walrus?

Iff You don't concentrate, do you? At P2C2E House there are many brilliant persons employed, but there is only one Grand Comptroller. They are the Eggheads. He is the Walrus. Got it now? Understood?

Haroun How does the letter get there?

Iff It doesn't. You see the beauty of the scheme?

Haroun Even if you do turn off your story water, my father will still be able to tell stories.

Iff Anybody can tell stories. Liars, and cheats, and crooks, for example. But for stories with that Extra Ingredient, ah, for those, even the best storytellers need the Story Waters. Storytelling needs fuel, just like a car; if you don't have the Water, you run out of Steam.

Haroun Why should I believe a word you say?

Iff Take the Disconnecting Tool, and just tap it against this space.

Haroun does this. The Disconnecting Tool makes a loud noise, just as if it has struck something extremely solid and extremely invisible.

There she blows. The Story Tap: *voilà*.

Haroun But I still don't get it. Where is this Ocean of yours? And how does the story water get into the tap? How does the plumbing work?
  Don't tell me. A Process Too Complicated To Explain.
  Mr Iff, you must take me to Gup City to see the Walrus, so I can get this stupid blunder about my father's Water supply reversed before it's too late.

Iff Impossible, no can do. Access to Gup City in Kahani, by the shores of the Ocean of the Streams of Story, is strictly restricted, completely forbidden, one hundred per cent banned, except to accredited personnel, like, for instance, me. But you? No chance, not in a million years, no way, José.

Haroun In that case you'll just have to go back without this.

Iff OK. If we're going, let's go.

Haroun You mean now?

Iff Now.

Haroun All right then, now.

Iff So pick a bird. Any bird.

Haroun The only bird here's a painted peacock.

Iff A person may choose what he cannot see.

A person may mention a bird's name even if the creature is not present and correct: crow, quail, hummingbird, bulbul, mynah, parrot, kite.

A person may even select a flying creature of his own invention, for example, winged horse, flying turtle, airborne whale, space serpent, aeromouse.

To give a thing a name, to rescue it from anonymity, to pluck it out of the Place of Namelessness – well, that's a way of bringing the said thing into being.

Haroun That may be true where you come from, but in these parts –

Iff In these parts I am having my time wasted by a Disconnector Thief who will not trust in what he can't see.

How much have you seen, eh, Thieflet?
Africa, have you seen it?
No? Then is it truly there?
And the past, did it happen?
And the future, will it come?
Believe in your own eyes and you'll get into a lot of trouble.
So take a look or, I should say, a gander . . .

Haroun Tiny birds were walking about on the Water Genie's palm, and pecking at it, and flapping their miniature wings to hover just above it. And as well as birds there were fabulous winged creatures out of legends: an Assyrian lion with the head of a bearded man and a pair of large hairy wings growing out of its flanks; and winged monkeys, flying saucers, tiny angels, levitating (and aparently air-breathing) fish.

Iff What's your pleasure, select, choose.

Haroun Haroun pointed at a tiny crested bird that was giving him a sidelong look through one highly intelligent eye.

Iff So it's the Hoopoe for us.
Perhaps you know, Disconnector Thief, that in the old stories the Hoopoe is the bird that leads all other birds through many dangerous places to their ultimate goal.
Well, well. Who knows, young Thieflet, who you may turn out to be.

Iff throws the Hoopoe through the window into the night.

23

Chorus Haroun saw the Hoopoe floating on the Dull Lake, as large as a double bed, easily large enough for a Water Genie and a boy to ride upon its back.

The Water Genie skips on to the Hoopoe's back – and Haroun is about to follow but pauses when he notices that the Hoopoe bears a startling resemblance to Mr Butt the bus driver.

Hoopoe No need to gawp like that, young sir, I can't help it if I remind you of someone.

Haroun You can read my mind. How are you doing that?

Hoopoe By a P2C2E. A Process Too Complicated To Explain.

Haroun I give up. (*He climbs aboard.*) Do you have a name?

Hoopoe Whatever name you please. But but but might I suggest, for obvious reasons, 'Butt'?

Iff And off we go!

All three take off and fly rapidly into the sky.

Haroun No bird can fly so fast. Is this a machine?

Hoopoe You maybe have some objection to machines? But but but you have entrusted your life to me. Then am I not worthy of a little of your respect?

The sun rises quickly. We see the Earth getting smaller in the distance behind them.

Chorus The sun rose and Haroun spotted something in the distance, a heavenly body like a large asteroid.

Hoopoe That is Kahani, the Earth's second moon.

Kahani increases in size as they approach.

Haroun But but but surely the Earth has just one Moon? How could a second satellite have remained undiscovered?

Hoopoe But but but it is because of Speed. The Moon, Kahani, travels so fast no Earth instruments can detect it.
  Moon approaching. Splashdown in ten seconds, nine, eight . . .

Chorus Rushing up towards them was a sparkling expanse of water.

Chorus And what water it was!

Chorus It shone with colours such as Haroun could never have imagined.

Haroun And it was warm; Haroun could see steam rising off it that glowed in the sunlight.

Iff The Ocean of the Streams of Story. Wasn't it worth travelling so far and fast to see?

Hoopoe Three, two, one, zero.

Splashdown.

Haroun It's a trick. There's no Gup City here, unless I'm very much mistaken. And no Gup City equals no P2C2E House, no Walrus, no point in being here at all.

Iff This is the Deep North of Kahani. We are here in search of Wishwater. When your wish is granted, you can return the Tool, and home you go to bed, and end of saga. OK?

Haroun Very well.

Iff And hey presto! Wishwater ahoy! (*He pulls out a small bottle with a little golden cap, which he fills with Wishwater and passes to Haroun.*) The harder you wish, the better it works.

So it's up to you.

Chorus Just one sip, and he could regain for his father the lost Gift of the Gab!

Haroun Down the hatch! (*He takes a swig from the bottle, which he puts away in a pocket.*)

Chorus Haroun began to focus his thoughts . . . He couldn't do it.

Chorus If he tried to concentrate on his father's lost storytelling powers and cancelled Story Water subscription, then the image of his mother insisted on taking over, and he began to wish for her return instead.

Haroun sees his father at the hands of the two unsmiling men from G, pleading with him.

Rashid Just do this one thing for me, my boy, just this one little thing.

And then Haroun sees his mother singing. And then his

father again. The two alternate, getting faster and
faster. Until with a sudden jangling noise, he is back
with Iff and the Hoopoe.

Iff Eleven minutes and his concentration goes, ka-bam, ka-blooey, ka-put.

Hoopoe But but but this is disgraceful, Iff. Wishes are not such easy things. You are upset because now we must go to Gup City after all, and there will be harsh words and hot water for you, and you are taking it out on the boy.

Iff Gup City it is. Unless, of course, you'd like to hand over the Disconnecting Tool and just call the whole thing off?

Hoopoe But but but you are still bullying the boy! Give the lad a happy story to drink.

Chorus So Iff the Water Genie told Haroun about the Ocean of the Streams of Story, and even though he was full of a sense of hopelessness and failure the magic of the Ocean began to have an effect on Haroun.

Chorus He looked into the water and saw that it was made up of a thousand thousand thousand and one different currents, each one a different colour, weaving in and out of one another like a liquid tapestry of breathtaking complexity; and each coloured strand represented and contained a single tale.

Chorus As all the stories ever told could be found here, the Ocean of the Streams of Story was in fact the biggest library in the universe.

Chorus And because the stories were in fluid form, they retained the ability to change, to join up with other stories and so become yet other stories.

Haroun So unlike a library of books, the Ocean of the Streams of Story isn't dead but alive.

Iff And if you are very, very careful, you can dip a cup into the Ocean, like so.

And you can fill it with water from a single, pure Stream of Story, like so.

And then you can offer it to a young fellow who's feeling blue, so the magic can restore his spirits.

Go on now; knock it back.

Haroun takes the golden cup and drinks.

Haroun Haroun found himself in a landscape that looked exactly like a giant chessboard, facing a white stone tower.

Chorus At the top of the tower was (what else but) a single window, out of which there gazed (who else but) a captive princess. Haroun as the hero was required to climb up the outside of the tower by clinging to the cracks between the stones with his bare hands and feet.

Haroun Halfway up the tower he noticed one of his hands beginning to change, becoming hairy, losing its human shape. (*He starts to change into a spider.*)

Princess Eek, my dearest, you have into a large spider turned.

> *As a spider Haroun makes rapid progress to the top of the tower; but when he reaches the window the princess produces a large carving knife and begins to hack and saw at his limbs, while chanting:*

Get away spider, go back home.

> *The Princess chops right through one of Haroun's arms and he falls. When he opens his eyes again he is lying full length on the back of Butt the Hoopoe.*

Iff It's pollution. Something, or somebody, has been putting filth into the Ocean. And if filth gets into the stories, they go wrong.
  If there are traces of this pollution right up here in the Deep North, things at Gup City must be close to crisis. This could mean war.

Haroun War with whom?

Hoopoe With the Land of Chup, on the Dark Side of Kahani.
  This looks like the doing of the leader of the Chupwalas, the Cultmaster of Bezaban.

Haroun And who's that?

Iff He is the Arch-Enemy of all Stories, even of Language

itself. He is the Prince of Silence and the Foe of Speech.
His name is Khattam-Shud.

Forked lightning glitters on the horizon.

Quick, quick! Top speed ahead.

12. JOURNEY TO GUP CITY

They begin speeding south to Gup City.

Hoopoe Thanks to the Eggheads at P2C2E House, the rotation of Kahani has been brought under control. The Land of Gup is bathed in Endless Sunshine, while over in Chup it's always the middle of the night. In between the two lies the Twilight Strip, in which Guppees long ago constructed an unbreakable and invisible Wall of Force. Its good name is Chattergy's Wall, after our King.

Haroun You're telling stories again.

Hoopoe Naturally I'm telling stories.

A large patch of what looks like a particularly thick type of weed or vegetable of some sort is racing along right beside them.

Haroun What's that?

Hoopoe A Floating Gardener, naturally.

Haroun You mean a Floating Garden.

Hoopoe That's all you know.

Now the high speed vegetation rears up out of the water and reveals that it is a man.

Mali Got a stranger with you. Very odd. Still. Your own business.

Haroun How do you do.

Mali Mali. Floating Gardener First Class. Who are you?

Haroun I'm Haroun. Please, what does a Floating Gardener do?

Mali Maintenance. Untwisting twisted Story Streams.

31

Weeding. In short: gardening.

Iff What's this pollution? When did it start? How bad is it?

Mali Lethal. Started only recently, but spread very rapid. Certain types of story may take years to clean up. Popular romances have become lists of shopping expeditions. Children's stories also. For instance, there is an outbreak of creatures with televisions in their stomachs.

The waters around them and the skies above fill up with mechanical birds.

Iff Something most serious has occurred. All units have been ordered back to base. Now if I had my Disconnecting Tool I would have received the order myself.

More new voices can be heard.

Goopy Hurry! Hurry! Don't be late!

Bagha Ocean's ailing! Cure can't wait!

Iff These are Plentimaw Fishes.

Haroun So, there really are Plentimaw Fish in the sea, just like Snooty Buttoo said.

Hoopoe Plentimaw Fishes always go in twos. They are faithful partners for life. To express this perfect union they speak in rhyme.

Bagha All this bad taste! Too much dirt!

Goopy Swimming in the Ocean starts to hurt!

Bagha Call me Bagha! This is Goopy!

Goopy Excuse our rudeness! We feel droopy!

Bagha Things are worse than we've ever known.

Goopy And the worst place is down in our Old Zone.

Iff claps his hand to his forehead.

Haroun What's wrong?

Iff The Old Zone is where the Source of Stories is located, from which the ancient stories flow. You know how people are – they want new things, always new. The old tales, nobody cares. But if the Source itself is poisoned, what will happen to the Ocean – to us all?

Hoopoe Hold on to hats. Hitting the brake now. Gup City dead ahead. No problem.

13. IT'S WAR

Large numbers of Guppees of an extraordinary thinness, dressed in entirely rectangular garments covered in writing, are marching in military manoeuvres.

Iff Those are the famous Pages of Gup; that is to say, the army. Ordinary armies are made up of platoons and regiments and suchlike; our Pages are organized into Chapters and Volumes. Each Volume is headed by a Front, or Title, Page; and there is the leader of the entire 'Library', our name for the army – General Kitab himself.

And that is Prince Bolo, the fiancé of King Chattergy's only child, his daughter the Princess Batcheat.

Bolo They have seized her, my Batcheat, my Princess. The servants of the Cultmaster purloined her some hours back. Churls, dastards, varlets, hounds! By gum, they will pay for this.

Kitab Her whereabouts are not known. Probably she will be kept prisoner in the Citadel of Chup, the Ice Castle of Khattam-Shud in Chup City, at the heart of the Perpetual Night.

We have sent messages to Cultmaster Khattam-Shud. These messages concerned both the vile poison being injected into the Ocean of the Streams of Story, and the abduction of Princess Batcheat. We demanded that he put a stop to the pollution and also return, within seven hours, the kidnapped Lady. Neither demand has been met. I have to inform you, therefore, that a state of war now exists between the Lands of Chup and Gup.

We hear a tannoy announcement.

Announcement Extreme urgency is of the essence. The poisons will destroy the entire Ocean if steps are not taken.

Iff Well, now it's war, young Thieflet. That means nobody at P2C2E House will have any time for your little request. You may as well hand back that Disconnecting Tool; then I'll have you taken home for nothing, completely free! There – what could be fairer than that?

Haroun No Walrus, no Disconnector. And that's flat.

Announcement Guppee patrols in the outlying areas of the Twilight Strip have arrested a highly suspicious person.

Pages lead on a man with his hands tied behind his back and a sack over his head. When the sack is removed, this man turns out to be Rashid.

Haroun Dad! What are you doing here?

Rashid Oh, goodness. Young Haroun. You are surely the most unexpected of boys.

Haroun He's not a spy. He's my father, and the only thing wrong with him is that he's lost the Gift of the Gab.

Rashid That's right. Go on, tell everyone, broadcast it to the whole world.

14. INTERROGATION

Rashid sits talking to General Kitab and Prince Bolo,
guarded by a Page, Blabbermouth. Iff and Haroun watch
them from a distance.

Haroun What do Guppees do to spies? Rip out their fin-
gernails one by one until they confess? Kill them slowly
and painfully?

Iff I don't know. We've never caught a spy before. Maybe
we should scold him. Or make him stand in a corner. Or
write 'I must not spy' one thousand and one times.

Rashid How I arrived in Gup, you will be wondering. It is
through certain dietary procedures. Certain foodstuffs,
properly prepared, will (a) induce sleep, but also (b) carry
the sleeper wherever he may wish. With sufficient skill, a
person may choose to wake up where the dream takes
him. I wished to travel to Gup; but owing to a slight direc-
tional miscalculation, I woke up in the Twilight Strip.

In the Twilight Strip I have heard bad things and seen
worse. There is an encampment there of the Chupwala
Army. Such black tents, wrapped in such a fanatical
silence! In the old days, the Cultmaster, Khattam-Shud,
preached hatred only towards stories and fancies and
dreams; but now he opposes speech for any reason at all.
The Land of Chup has fallen under the 'Mystery of
Bezaban', a cult whose followers swear vows of lifelong
silence. Bezaban is a gigantic idol at the heart of Khattam-
Shud's citadel carved out of black ice. It has no tongue
but grins frightfully, showing teeth the size of houses.

Why should I wait near that awful camp? I went
towards the distant light on the horizon and came to
Chattergy's Wall; sirs, it is in bad repair. There are many
holes, movement through it is easily achieved. The

Chupwalas know this – I saw them – I witnessed the kidnapping of Batcheat with my own eyes!

Bolo Why have you waited so long to tell us? Zounds! Proceed; for pity's sake.

Rashid I was struggling through the tangles of thornbushes, when a swan-boat of silver and gold approached. In it was a young woman with long hair, wearing a circlet of gold, and singing, please excuse, the ugliest sounding song I have ever heard. In addition her teeth, her nose . . .

Kitab You needn't go on.

Bolo Batcheat, Batcheat! Shall I never hear your sweet sweet voice, or gaze upon your delicate face again?

Rashid She was with her handmaidens. They were giggling about Chattergy's Wall, wanting to go up and touch it. 'I want to know what it's like,' I heard her say. 'If the eye can't see it, maybe the finger can feel, maybe the tongue can taste.' Just then a Chupwala party came through a hole in the Wall, seized the Princess and her handmaidens and carried them off towards the tents of Chup.

Bolo And what kind of man are you, that you stayed hidden and did nothing to save them from such a fate?

Haroun How dare he?

Iff ·Princes can get like that. Don't worry. We don't let him do anything important.

Rashid What would you have preferred? That I, unarmed and half-dead with cold, should have leapt like a romantic fool from my hiding place, and got myself captured or killed? Then who would have brought you the news – who would be able, now, to show you the way to the Chupwala encampment?

Kitab You should apologize, Bolo.

Bolo I was too sharp. Truly, we are grateful for your news.

Rashid There's one thing more. As the Chupwala soldiers hauled the Princess away, I heard them say: 'The Great Feast of Bezaban is coming soon. Why not, on the day, offer our Idol this Guppee Princess as a sacrifice? We'll stitch up her lips and rename her the Dumb Princess – the Princess Khamosh.' Then they laughed.

A hush falls over the room.

Bolo Now there is not a second to lose! Assemble the armed forces – all the Pages, every Chapter, every Volume! To war, to war! For Batcheat!

Kitab For Batcheat and the Ocean!

Bolo Yes, yes. The Ocean also; naturally, of course, very well.

Rashid If you wish, I will lead you to the Chupwala tents.

Bolo Good man. I did you wrong; you're a champion.

Haroun If you're going, don't think you can leave me behind.

Haroun's body is possessed by a magnificent yawn.

Rashid Could you find my son a bed for the night?

Kitab (*instructing a Page to do as Rashid asks*) Blabbermouth.

Haroun I'm not sleepy, really I'm not.

Rashid leaves with Bolo, Kitab and Iff. Haroun is left on his own with Blabbermouth.

38

Haroun Blabbermouth led Haroun along corridors, up staircases, down staircases, along more corridors, through doorways, around corners, into courtyards, out of court-yards, on to balconies and down corridors again.

Blabbermouth If my fiancée got herself kidnapped because she was crazy enough to go into the Twilight Strip just to go gooey over the stars in the sky and touch the stupid Wall for goodness' sake, don't imagine I'd start a war to get her back; I'd say good riddance, especially with her nose, her teeth, and I haven't even mentioned her singing, you wouldn't believe how horrible, and now instead of letting her rot we're all going to go in after her and probably get ourselves killed because we won't be able to see properly in the dark –

Haroun Are we getting to my bedroom soon?

Blabbermouth And these uniforms, have you read this?

Haroun Bolo and the Golden Fleece?

Blabbermouth Whose idea do you think that was? Hers, obviously, Batcheat's, she had all the greatest stories in the world rewritten as if her Bolo was the hero or something and we have to walk round wearing them; Bolo and the Wonderful Lamp, Bolo and the Forty Thieves, Bolo and Juliet, Bolo in Wonderland –

Haroun We're lost, aren't we?

Blabbermouth So we're a little lost, but aren't we having a nice chat?

> *Haroun knocks the cap off Blabbermouth's head, thereby unexpectedly revealing a great torrent of shiny black hair.*

What did you do that for? Now you've spoilt everything.

Haroun You're a girl.

Blabbermouth Shhh. You want me to get the sack? You think it's easy for a girl to get a job like this? Don't you know girls have to fool people every day of their lives if they want to get anywhere?

Haroun You mean just because you're a girl you aren't allowed to be a Page?

Blabbermouth I suppose you only do what you're told. I suppose you always eat up all the food on your plate, even the cauliflower.

Haroun At least I could do something perfectly simple like showing someone where their bedroom is.

Blabbermouth I suppose you always go to bed when you're told to. And you wouldn't be at all interested in going up on to the palace roof through this secret passageway right here.

Blabbermouth pushes a button and takes Haroun up a hidden staircase.

Chorus Haroun sat on the flat roof of the palace in what was still, of course, dazzling sunshine, and gazed out at the view of the Land of Gup.

Chorus The gigantic formal gardens with fountains and pleasure-domes and ancient spreading trees, which swept right down in terraces to the water's edge.

Chorus The Lagoon, a beautiful expanse of multi-coloured waters, in which a great flotilla of mechanical birds was assembling.

Chorus And out across the endangered Ocean of the Streams of Story.

Haroun Haroun realized, quite suddenly, that he had never felt more completely alive in his life, even if he was ready to drop with fatigue.

Without a word, Blabbermouth takes three soft balls made of golden silk from one of her pockets, tosses them into the air so that they catch the sunlight, and begins to juggle.

She juggles behind her back, over and under her leg, with her eyes closed, and lying down, juggling more and more balls until Haroun is speechless with admiration.

Blabbermouth stops juggling.

Haroun has fallen asleep.

Blabbermouth takes the Disconnecting Tool out of Haroun's hand and leaves.

Interval.

Haroun is still sleeping. Blabbermouth enters and grabs him by the throat.

Blabbermouth Rise and Shine.

As Haroun wakes he realizes he is being strangled and tries to free himself, but Blabbermouth is stronger.

If you tell anyone about me, next time I won't stop squeezing.

Haroun concedes defeat and Blabbermouth releases him.

Haroun I won't tell, I promise.

Blabbermouth You're OK, Haroun Khalifa.

Haroun basks in Blabbermouth's approval. After a pause, he slowly starts looking for something.

By the way, I took the liberty of returning that Disconnector you stole.

Haroun I thought you were my friend.

Blabbermouth Your father's here himself now, he can sort out his own problem.

Haroun You don't get it. I wanted to do it for him.

They are interrupted by a fanfare of trumpets.

Blabbermouth Time to report for duty.

17. THE TASK FORCE ASSEMBLES

Pages and other Guppees rush about in a most disorderly fashion. Haroun and Blabbermouth scramble to join them. They meet Iff, Butt the Hoopoe, Rashid, Mali, Goopy, Bagha, Prince Bolo and General Kitab. Finally, everyone is ready.

Kitab For Batcheat and the Ocean.

All For Batcheat and the Ocean.

> *They set off. Gradually, Guppee conversation gets louder and louder.*

Bagha Saving Batcheat! What a notion!

Goopy What matters is to save the Ocean!

Mali It's a Wild Goose Chase to go after Batcheat!

Blabbermouth Yes, and she looks like a Wild Goose too.

Bagha That's the plan to set in motion –

Goopy – find the source of the Poison Potion!

Kitab How dare you? That's our beloved Princess you're talking about; our estimable Prince Bolo's intended and beauteous bride!

Iff Beauteous? Have you forgotten that voice, that nose, those teeth?

Haroun What an army! If any soldiers behaved like this on Earth, they'd be court-martialled quick as thinking.

Hoopoe But but but what is the point of giving persons freedom of Speech, if you then say they must not utilize same? And is not the Power of Speech the greatest Power of all? Then surely it must be exercized to the full?

Bolo Only Prince Bolo remained aloof, saying nothing, looking neither to left nor right, his eyes fixed on the far horizon. For him there was no argument: Batcheat came first; the issue was beyond dispute.

Haroun How can Bolo be so certain, when every other Guppee seems to take for ever to make his mind up about anything?

Mali It is Love. Which is a wonderful and dashing matter. But which can also be a very foolish thing.

Rashid The light failed slowly, then more quickly.

Haroun They were in the Twilight Strip!

Blabbermouth The closer they came to the shores of the Land of Chup, the more formidable the prospect of the Chupwala Army became.

Hoopoe On those twilit shores, no bird sang.

Goopy No wind blew.

Bagha No voice spoke.

Bolo Feet falling on shingle made no sound, as if the pebbles were coated in some unknown muffling material.

Kitab The air smelt stale and stenchy.

Iff All was stillness and cold.

Haroun The silence and darkness seemed content to bide their time.

Rashid stops and points.

Rashid There was a small clearing up ahead, and in this leafless glade was a man who looked almost like a shadow, and who held a sword whose blade was dark as night.

Iff The man was alone, but turned and leapt and kicked and slashed his sword constantly, as though battling an invisible opponent.

Haroun Then Haroun saw that the man was actually fighting against his own shadow; which, in turn, was fighting back.

Blabbermouth The shadow plainly possessed a will of its own.

The Warrior and his shadow continue fighting. Then suddenly the Warrior stiffens and walks slowly towards the Guppee party. His hands move furiously in something like a dance of rage or hate. His hand movements become faster and faster, more and more emphatic until suddenly he lets his hands drop and begins to speak.

Mudra Gogogol. Kafkafka.

Bolo Eh? What's that? What's the fellow saying? Can't make out a single word.

Rashid If people in the Land of Chup hardly talk at all these days then it's hardly surprising he's lost control of his voice.

Bolo Really, why people can't speak properly, it beats me.

Mudra Murder. Spock Obi New Year.

Bolo So it's murder he plans. Well, he won't have it all his own way, I promise him that.

Kitab Bolo, dash it all, will you be quiet? He's trying to tell us something.

Mudra Murder. Murder. Spock Obi New Year.

Rashid I've got it. What a fool I am. He's been talking to us fluently all the time. It's the hand movements. He has been using the Language of Gesture. What he said wasn't 'murder', but Mudra. That's his name. Mudra. Speak Abhinaya. That's what he's been saying. 'Abhinaya' is the name of the most ancient Gesture Language of all, which it just so happens I know.

Mudra and his Shadow instantly begin nodding furiously. The Shadow starts to use Gesture Language as rapidly as Mudra himself.

Rashid Hang on. One at a time please.

Nothing to worry about. Mudra is a friend. Also, this is lucky – the Champion Warrior of Chup, second in authority only to Cultmaster Khattam-Shud himself.

Bolo We really are in luck. Let's seize him, put him in chains and tell the Cultmaster we'll only release him if we get Batcheat back safe and sound.

Kitab And how do you propose to capture him?

Rashid Please listen. Mudra has become disgusted with the cruelty and fanaticism of the Cult of Bezaban, and has broken off relations with Khattam-Shud. I'll interpret his Abhinaya for you.

(Rashid) (*interpreting what Mudra is 'saying' with his hands*) Don't think all Chupwalas follow Khattam-Shud or worship Bezaban. Mostly they are simply terrified. If he were defeated, the people in Chup would turn to me; my Shadow and I are both in favour of Peace.

Now the Shadow 'speaks'.

(Rashid) In Chup, Shadows are the equals of the people to whom they are joined. They learn to change simply by wishing to do so. A shadow very often has a stronger personality than the person and of course there can be quarrels; they can pull in opposite directions. Among the Shadows, Cultmaster Khattam-Shud has made terrible trouble.

Mudra resumes the narrative.

(Rashid) He has become like a shadow and his Shadow more like a person. It goes wherever it wishes. The Cultmaster can be in two places at once!

Blabbermouth But that's the worst news in the world! It was going to be almost impossible to defeat him once – and now you tell us we'll have to beat him twice?

(Rashid) Precisely so.

47

A silence falls.

Bolo Why should we believe this creature? How do we know this isn't some sort of trap?

Kitab Your highness, I am in command here. Hold your tongue or you'll be on your way back to Gup City, and someone else will have to rescue your Batcheat on your behalf; and you wouldn't like that, spots and fogs, you wouldn't.

Mudra's Shadow responds to Bolo's outburst by going into a positive frenzy of changes, growing enormous, scratching itself all over, turning into the silhouette of a flame-breathing dragon. While the Shadow behaves in this agitated fashion, Mudra himself pretends to have grown very bored indeed. General Kitab approaches Mudra with great respect.

Will you help us? It isn't going to be easy in the Darkness of Chup. We could do with a fellow like you. What do you say?

(Rashid) Yes, I will help. The Cultmaster must be defeated. But there is a decision you must make.

Blabbermouth I know what it is. It's the same one we should have made before we even set out: who do we save first? Batcheat or the Ocean?

By the way, isn't he something? Isn't he wicked, awesome, sharp? Mudra, I mean.

Haroun I know who you mean. He's OK, I suppose.

Blabbermouth OK? Only OK?

(Rashid) There are two Khattam-Shuds. One has Princess Batcheat in the Citadel of Chup, and plans to sew up her lips. The other is in the Old Zone, where he is plotting to ruin the Ocean of the Streams of Story.

Bolo A Person must come before an Ocean, no matter how great the peril to both! What are you people? Have you not blood in your veins? General, and you too, Sir Mudra, are you men or . . . or . . . shadows?

Mudra's Shadow gestures with quiet dignity.

(Rashid) There is no need to insult shadows any further.

Kitab Rot it all, very well. But we must send someone to the Old Zone. Let me see . . .

Haroun I'll go.

Bolo What's that you say?

Kitab Why d'you volunteer for this dangerous job?

Haroun All my life I've heard about the wonderful Sea of Stories and Water Genies and everything, but I didn't really believe in them until I saw Iff in my bathroom the other night. And now that I've actually come to Kahani and seen with my own eyes how beautiful the Ocean is, and its Floating Gardeners and Plentimaw Fishes, it turns out I may be too late, because the whole Ocean's going to be dead in a minute if we don't do something. I don't like the idea that all the good stories in the world will go wrong for ever and ever, or die. Maybe it isn't too late for me to do my bit.

Rashid There's more to you, young Haroun Khalifa, than meets the blinking eye.

Bolo General, I ask you: is this not the perfect fellow for the job? For he is, like me, a slave to Love.
  Just as my great passion, my Amour, leads me towards Batcheat, always towards Batcheat, so this boy's destiny is to rescue what he loves: that is, the Ocean of Stories.

Haroun avoids looking at Blabbermouth, and blushes.

Kitab Very well, young master Haroun, you will be our spy. Take your pick of companions, and begone.

Haroun is travelling on Butt the Hoopoe, together with Iff, Goopy, Bagha and Mali.

Bagha We're going the right way! We can tell!

Goopy Before it was filthy! Now it's Hell!

Haroun If that water is so badly poisoned, doesn't it hurt your feet?

Mali Take more 'n that. A little poison, bah. A little acid, pah. A Gardener's a tough old bird. It won't stop me.
 You can stop a cheque
 You can stop a leak or three
 You can stop traffic, but
 You can't stop me!

They come to a halt.

Haroun What we are here to stop is the work of the Cultmaster, Khattam-Shud.

Iff If it's true that there is a Wellspring, or Source of Stories, near the South Pole, then that's where Khattam-Shud will be, you can be sure of it.

Haroun Very well, then. To the South Pole!

They start moving again.

Goopy I feel terrible! She feels worse!

Bagha We can hardly speak in verse.

Haroun Whatever is doing this can't be very far away. Stay here and keep watch. We'll go on without you.

Goopy and Bagha are left behind as the others continue on their journey. A weed jungle forms in front of them.

51

Iff Look at the Ocean. The oldest stories ever made, and look at them now. We let them rot, we abandoned them, long before this poisoning. Boring, we said, surplus to requirements. And now, look, just look! No colour, no life, no nothing. Spoilt!

Haroun Surely there's not meant to be any land here?

Mali Neglected waters is what it is. Nobody to keep the place in trim. It's a disgrace. Bit of weeding. Bit of pest control. Have a channel ready in no time.

Huge clumps of vegetation fly into the air as Mali gets to work. The creatures who live in the weed jungle rush out in alarm.

Haroun Mali? Where have you got to?

There is no reply. One of the Water Genie's attractively embroidered and twirly-pointed slippers falls into the Ocean, where, quick as a blink, with a fizz and a hiss and a burble and a gurgle, it is instantly eaten away. A hissing sound can be heard, and an instant later something enormous is thrown in their direction – like a colossal net spun out of darkness itself.

Hoopoe It's a Web of Night. A legendary Chupwala weapon. The more you fight, the harder it grips. To Khattam-Shud we go, all neatly wrapped and tied-up like a present! It's finito for us all.

Haroun Honestly, Hoopoe, pull yourself together.

Hoopoe How to pull myself, together or anywhere else, when other persons, Chupwala persons, are pulling me wherever they desire?

The Web of Night is pulled away. We see a row of black portholes.

Haroun That's where they'll be taking us: the Flagship of Khattam-Shud!

> *Darkness pours out of the portholes – glowing in the twilight the way light does from a window in the evening.*

The Chupwalas have invented artificial darkness, just like other people have artificial light!

> *A party of Chupwalas surround Butt the Hoopoe, climb on to Butt's back and unscrew the top of the Hoopoe's head.*

Hoopoe But but but that you must not take – no, you can't – it's my brain!

> *Emitting a series of short, satisfied hisses, they remove a small, metal box from the head cavity.*
> *Butt the Hoopoe is left simply floating there, its memory cells and command module removed.*
> *While this is happening, Iff grabs Haroun's hand and pushes something into his palm.*

Iff A little emergency something, courtesy of P2C2E House. Maybe you'll get a chance to use it.

Haroun What is it?

Iff Bite the end off and it gives you two full minutes of bright, bright light. So it's called a Bite-a-Lite, for obvious reasons. Hide it under your tongue.

> *Chupwalas come and lead them away.*

Haroun Oh, Hoopoe, you're the best and bravest machine that ever there was, and I'll get your brain back for you, just see if I don't.

Haroun and Iff are brought on by Chupwalas. A crane towers above the deck like a tall building and from its mighty arm immense chains descend into the waters.

Haroun It's a factory ship and what it makes is far, far worse than the sadness factories back home.

Enter Khattam-Shud.

Khattam-Shud Spies. What a tiresome melodrama. A Water Genie from Gup City, and something more unusual, a young fellow, if I'm not mistaken, from down there.

Iff So much for all your silence nonsense. Isn't it typical, wouldn't you have known: his followers sew up their lips and he talks and talks like billy-o.

Khattam-Shud ignores these remarks.
The Chupwala who removed Butt the Hoopoe's brain-box gives this to Khattam-Shud.

Khattam-Shud Now we shall see about their Processes Too Complicated To Explain. Once this is taken apart, I'll explain those processes, never fear.

Haroun I know him. I've met him somewhere before.

Khattam-Shud What brought you here, eh? Stories, I suppose. Well, look where stories have landed you now. You'd have done better to stick to Facts. Stories make trouble. Answer me this: what's the use of stories that aren't even true?

Haroun You're him. You're Mr Sengupta and you stole my mother and you left the fat lady behind and you're a snivelling, drivelling, mingy, stingy, measly, weasely clerk.

Where are you hiding her? Maybe she's a prisoner on this ship! Come on; hand her over.

Iff Haroun, it's not the same guy. Maybe he looks the same, but, believe me, this is the Cultmaster of Bezaban, Khattam-Shud.

Khattam-Shud Stories have warped the boy's brain. Why would I have the slightest interest in your mother? Stories have made you incapable of seeing who stands before you. Stories have made you believe that a Personage such as the Cultmaster Khattam-Shud ought to look like . . . this.

> *The Cultmaster grows and grows until he is one hundred and one feet tall, with one hundred and one heads, each of which has three eyes and a protruding tongue of flame; and a hundred and one arms, one hundred of which are holding enormous black swords, while the one hundred and first tosses Butt the Hoopoe's brainbox casually in the air.*
>
> *Then, with a little sigh, Khattam-Shud shrinks back into his earlier, clerkish form.*

Showing off.
Well, you must see what you came to see. Though obviously you will not be able to make your report. Bring them.

Below decks, the Dark Ship is full of machinery.
  And what machines they are!
  Far Too Complicated To Describe.
  What a whizzing of whirrers and stirring of stirrers,
what ranks of lifters and banks of sifters, what a hum-
ming of squeezers and frumming of freezers is there!

Khattam-Shud These are the poison blenders. We must
make a great many poisons because every story in the
Ocean needs to be ruined in a different way. To ruin a
happy story, you must make it sad. To ruin an action
drama, you must make it move too slowly. To ruin a mystery you must make the criminal's identity obvious even
to the most stupid audience.

I personally have discovered that for every story there is
an anti-story. And if you pour this anti-story into the
story, the two cancel each other out and bingo! End of
story. Each day we synthesize and release new poisons!
Each day we murder new tales! Soon the Ocean will be
dead, my victory will be complete.

Haroun But why do you hate stories so much? Stories are
fun . . .

Khattam-Shud The world, however, is not for Fun. The
world is for Controlling.

Haroun Which world?

Khattam-Shud Your world, my world, all worlds. They
are all there to be Ruled. And inside every single story,
inside every Stream in the Ocean, there lies a world, a
story world, I cannot Rule at all. And that is the reason
why.

Haroun Look at the edges of everything here. Don't they look, well, fuzzy? That's what shadows are like; even when they're sharp, they're never as sharp-edged as real, substantial things. This is the Cultmaster's Shadow. He has sent the Shadow here, and remains in the Citadel of Chup.

Khattam-Shud Now this is where we are building the Plug.

Iff What Plug? You can't mean . . .

Khattam-Shud You will have seen the giant crane up on deck. You will have noted the chains going down into the waters. At the other end of those chains, Chupwala divers are rapidly assembling the largest and most efficient Plug ever constructed. We are going to plug the Wellspring itself, the Source of Stories. As long as that Source remains unplugged, fresh, unpoisoned, renewing Story Waters will pour into the Ocean. But when it's Plugged! Ah, then what will there be for you Guppees to do, but accept the victory of Bezaban?

Haroun How do the divers enter the poisoned waters without being hurt?

Khattam-Shud They wear protective clothing. Here, in this cupboard, are numbers of poison-proof suits. And this is our Generator.

Through an open porthole a few paces from the Cultmaster, bizarre rooty tendrils begin to enter the Dark Ship.

Haroun Mali!

Iff puts his hand over Haroun's mouth.

Khattam-Shud Intruder! Intruder alert!

Mali flings roots and tendrils all over the Generator, getting into every nook and cranny. The ship's entire power supply is cut off at once.

*Stirrers stop stirring and whirrers stop whirring;
blenders stop blending and menders stop mending;
squeezers stop squeezing and freezers stop freezing; poison-storers stop storing and poison-pourers stop pouring.*

*Chupwala guards now attack Mali in great numbers,
pulling at him with their bare hands, hacking at him
with axes and swords; but he hangs on to the Generator
until he is sure it is ruined beyond hope of quick repair.*

Mali

You can chop a flower-bush
You can chop a tree
You can chop liver, but
You can't chop me!
You can chop and change
You can chop in ka-ra-tee
You can chop suey, but
You can't chop me!

Iff The Bite-a-Lite!

Quickly, Haroun puts it between his teeth, and bites.

*The Chupwalas all around him are blinded, and
break their vows of silence to utter curses as they clutch
their eyes. Even Khattam-Shud reels back from the
glare.*

*Haroun takes the Bite-a-Lite out of his mouth and
holds it over his head; light pours in every direction.*

*As he passes Khattam-Shud, he grabs Butt the
Hoopoe's brain-box from the Cultmaster's hand.*

*He runs on, until he reaches the cupboard containing
the protective clothing for the Chupwala divers.*

*With Iff's help, Haroun zips up the diving suit, pulls
on the goggles and, just as the two minutes of light
come to an end, dives head-first out of a porthole.*

23. THE SOURCE OF STORIES

Haroun, in the diving suit, is now underwater.

Haroun The deeper Haroun went, the less filthy the Story Streams were, and the easier it was to see.

He saw the Plug.

And then, wonder of wonders, he caught sight of the Source itself.

The Source of Stories was a hole in the sea-bed, and through that hole the glowing flow of pure, unpolluted stories came bubbling up from the very heart of Kahani.

There are so many Streams of Story, of so many different colours, that the source looks like a huge underwater fountain of shining white light.

In that moment Haroun understood that if he could prevent the Source from being Plugged, everything would eventually be all right again.

The renewed Streams of Story would cleanse the polluted waters, and Khattam-Shud's plan would fail.

Oh, I wish, how I wish, there was something I could do.

His hand brushes against his diving-suit and he feels a bulge in the pocket underneath.

That's strange, I'm sure I put Butt the Hoopoe's brain-box in the pocket on the other side.

Then he remembered what was in that pocket, and in a flash he knew that there was something he could do after all.

Haroun surfaces right next to the disabled Butt the Hoopoe. He climbs aboard stealthily, lifts the lid, and looks inside. There are three loose leads. But which goes where?

Haroun Here goes!

Haroun wires up the Hoopoe.

Hoopoe
You must sing, a-down, a-down,
And you call him a-down-a.

Haroun I've sent it insane. (*He tries again.*)

Hoopoe Look, look. A mouse. This piece of toasted cheese will do it.

Haroun Hoopoe, be quiet, please. (*He disconnects the three leads and changes them round.*)

Hoopoe So what took you so long? All fixed up now, let's go. Va-va-voom!

Haroun Hold your horses, Hoopoe. Just sit there and pretend you're still brainless. I've got something else to do. (*He reaches into his other nightshirt pocket and draws out the bottle still half-full of Wishwater.*)
Wishwater.
The harder you wish, the better it works.
I'm going to do it all right. Hoopoe, you just watch me try. (*He drinks the Wishwater down to the last drop.*) I wish, I wish this Moon, Kahani, to turn, so that it's no longer half in light and half in darkness . . . I wish it to turn, this very instant, in such a way that the sun shines down on the Dark Ship, the full, hot, noonday sun.

Hoopoe That's some wish. This will be pretty interesting.

Haroun stretches out, with his eyes tight shut, concentrating.

A dark beam from the torch of a Chupwala searcher picks him out.

The search party race towards Butt the Hoopoe as fast as they can go.

And then, with a mighty shuddering and a mighty juddering, the Moon Kahani turns – quickly, as Haroun had specified during his wishing – and the sun rises, at high speed, and zooms up into the sky until it is directly overhead, where it remains.

Haroun What do you know? I did it! I actually managed to get it done.

Hoopoe Never doubted you for a moment.

The Chupwala searchers racing towards Haroun shriek and hiss as the sunlight hits them; they grow fuzzy at the edges, and begin, it seems, to melt and then sizzle away altogether . . .

Haroun Look. Look what's happening to the ship!

The ship itself has started to melt.

Iff! Mali!

Iff and Mali are prisoners in the rapidly sinking ship. However, as everything on the ship is a shadow – including their shackles – they succeed in freeing themselves and come to join Haroun and Butt the Hoopoe.

Haroun Let's get out of here. Hoopoe, full speed ahead!

Butt the Hoopoe moves rapidly towards the channel which Mali had cut in the weed-jungle.

Iff With a strange, sad, sucking sound, the Dark Ship of Cultmaster Khattam-Shud finally melted right away.

Mali And the Plug, incomplete as it was, fell harmlessly on to the ocean-bed, leaving the Source of Stories entirely unblocked-up.

Haroun Fresh stories would go on pouring out of it, and so, one day, the Ocean would be clean again, and all the stories, even the oldest ones, would taste as good as new.

There is an unhealthy sounding noise, and they come to an abrupt halt.

Iff He's blown a fuse.

Rashid Now I must tell you quickly about everything that happened while Haroun was away in the Old Zone.

Chorus Princess Batcheat Chattergy, you will remember, was being held prisoner in the topmost room of the topmost tower of the Citadel of Chup.

Chorus Chup City was in the deep heart of the Perpetual Darkness, and the air was so cold that it would freeze into icicles on people's noses, and hang there until it was broken off.

Chorus For this reason, the Chupwalas who lived there wore little spherical nosewarmers that gave them the look of circus clowns, except that the nosewarmers were black.

Chorus Red nosewarmers were issued to the Pages of Gup as they marched into the Darkness.

Rashid Really, this is beginning to look like a war between buffoons.

Kitab The Guppee commanders sat down to a light pre-battle dinner in their tent; and while they were eating a Chupwala ambassador rode up, carrying a white flag of truce.

Bolo Well, Chupwala, what's your business?

Ambassador The High Cultmaster, Khattam-Shud, has granted me special release from my vows of silence. He sends you greetings and informs you that you are all trespassing on the sacred soil of Chup. He will neither negotiate with you, nor give up your spying nosy-parker of a Batcheat – and, oh, but she's noisy too. She torments our ears with her songs! And as for her nose, her teeth . . .

Kitab There's no need to go into that. We aren't interested in your opinions.

Ambassador Unless you retreat at once, your invasion will be punished by annihilation. However, before your utter defeat, I am commanded to entertain you for a moment. I am, if I may immodestly say it, the finest juggler in Chup City, and am ordered to juggle for your delight.

Blabbermouth Don't trust him – it's a trick.

Bolo Silence, Page! The rules of chivalry demand our acceptance!

> *The Ambassador begins his performance.*
> *From the depths of his cloak he produces a bewildering variety of objects and flings them into mesmerizing hoops and whirls.*
> *His audience is so completely hypnotized by his skill that only one person sees the moment at which one extra object is added to the flying cavalcade, a little, heavy rectangular box out of which protrudes a short, burning fuse . . .*

Blabbermouth Will you for Pete's sake look out? The guy's got a live bomb!

> *Blabbermouth plucks the bomb right out of the dancing array of objects in the air and throws it away while others grab the Chupwala, whose juggled objects fall to the floor.*
> *Blabbermouth's helmet falls off in her exertions – her hair falls about her shoulders for all to see.*

I told you it was a trick.

Bolo What's this, Blabbermouth? Are you a girl? You're fired.

Kitab Bolo, hang it all.

Blabbermouth Oh no, I'm not. Mister, I quit.

Mudra intervenes.

(Rashid) We must not quarrel when the battle is about to begin. If Prince Bolo has no further need of so courageous a Page, then perhaps Miss Blabbermouth would care to work for me?

Bolo looks crestfallen and Blabbermouth looks exceptionally pleased.

27. THE BATTLE

Chorus The battle was joined at last.

Rashid Rashid Khalifa, watching the action from the Guppee Command hill, was very much afraid that the Pages of Gup would be beaten badly. Torn up, or perhaps burned.

Chorus The Guppees were still busily arguing over every little detail.

Chorus But then the Chupwalas were quite unable to resist the Guppees.

Chorus All those arguments and debates, all that openness, had created powerful bonds of fellowship between them.

Chorus The Chupwalas, on the other hand, turned out to be a disunited rabble.

Chorus Their habits of secrecy had made them suspicious and distrustful of one another.

Chorus They did not stand shoulder to shoulder, but betrayed one another, stabbed one another in the back, mutinied, hid, deserted . . . and after the shortest clash imaginable, simply threw down all their weapons and ran away.

28. LIBERATION OF CHUP

Chorus The army or 'Library' of Gup entered Chup City in triumph.

Chorus Chupwala maidens rushed black-nosed into the icy streets and garlanded the red-nosed Guppees with black snowdrops, and kissed them, too, and called them 'Liberators of Chup'.

Chorus And now, wafting down to them from the Citadel came a woman's voice singing songs of love.

Rashid It was the most horrible voice Rashid Khalifa, the Shah of Blah, had heard in all his life.

Batcheat
Oooh I'm talking 'bout my Bolo
And I ain't got time for nothin' else!

Bolo Beautiful! That's so beautiful!

Batcheat
Lemme tell you 'bout a boy I know,
He's my Bolo and I love him so!

Bolo Just listen to that. Is that a voice or what is it?

All It must be a what is it. Because a voice it certainly is not.

Chorus At that moment a miracle happened.

Chorus The ground shook beneath their feet.

Chorus The houses of Chup trembled; many Chupwalas (and Guppees too) cried out in terror.

Chorus Prince Bolo fell off his horse.

All Look at the sky!

Chorus The sun was rising over Chup City, over the Citadel of Chup.

Chorus It was rising rapidly, and went on rising until it was directly overhead, blazing down in the full fury of its noonday heat; and there it stayed.

Chorus The black ice of that dark fortress received the sunlight like a mortal wound.

Chorus The locks on the Citadel gates melted away.

Chorus Bolo ran with Mudra up flights of stairs and through courtyards, while all around them the pillars of Khattam-Shud's Citadel began to buckle and bend.

Bolo Batcheat!

Batcheat (*off*) Bolo!

Chorus The shadowless servants of the Cultmaster, the members of the Union of the Zipped Lips, were running blindly hither and yon, smashing into walls, knocking one another out as they collided, and shrieking dreadfully, all Laws of Silence forgotten in their fear.

Chorus And at last, the Princess Batcheat came into sight, with that nose, those teeth . . . But there's no need to go into that.

Bolo Batcheat!

Batcheat Bolo!

> *It is indeed Batcheat, sliding down the banister of a grand staircase whose steps have melted away.*
>   *Bolo waits.*
>   *Batcheat flies off the banister into his arms.*
>   *He staggers backwards, but does not fall.*

Chorus High above them, at the very apex of the Citadel, the gigantic ice-statue, of tongueless, grinning,

69

many-toothed Bezaban was beginning to totter and shake; and then, drunkenly, it fell.

Rashid Look!

An unimpressive little figure in a hooded cloak had come scurrying out.

Chorus A skinny, scrawny, snivelling, drivelling, mingy, stingy, measily, weaselly, clerkish sort of fellow, who had no shadow but seemed almost as much a shadow as a man.

Rashid It was the Cultmaster, Khattam-Shud, running for his life.

Chorus He heard Rashid's cry too late; whirled around with a fiendish yell; and saw the huge head of the Colossus of Bezaban as it arrived, hitting him squarely on the nose.

Chorus Not a shred of him was ever seen again.

Chorus Peace broke out.

Mudra The new government of the Land of Chup, headed by Mudra, announced its desire for a long and lasting peace with Gup, a peace in which Night and Day, Speech and Silence, would no longer be separated into Zones by Twilight Strips and Walls of Force.

Blabbermouth Mudra invited Miss Blabbermouth to stay with him, to act as go-between for the Guppee authorities and those of Chup; and Blabbermouth accepted gladly.

Haroun Haroun was reunited with his father, who was given back his Story Water facilities and awarded the Land of Gup's highest decoration, the Order of the Open Mouth, in recognition of his exceptional services during the war.

Iff Iff was named Chief Water Genie, Mali Head Floating Gardener and Goopy and Bagha Leaders of all the Plentimaw Fishes in the Sea.

Hoopoe Butt the Hoopoe was quickly restored to his normal self, just as soon as the Gup Service Station had fitted it with a spare brain.

Batcheat And Princess Batcheat?

Rashid On the day of her wedding to Prince Bolo, the two of them looked so happy and so much in love that everyone decided to forget about how incredibly idiotic Batcheat had been to get herself captured in the first place, and about Bolo's many pieces of foolish behaviour during the war that followed.

Kitab A great victory has been won, a victory for our Ocean over its Enemy, but also a victory for the new

Friendship and Openness between Chup and Gup, over our old Hostility and Suspicion. A dialogue has been opened; and to celebrate that, as well as this wedding, let all the people sing.

Rashid Batcheat kept her mouth shut and everyone was as happy as could be.

After the others have dispersed, Haroun is approached by an Egghead.

Egghead You're to present yourself at once at P2C2E House. The Walrus wants to talk to the person who destroyed so much irreplaceable machinery.

Haroun But it was in a good cause.

Egghead I don't know about that.

30. HAROUN'S THIRD WISH

Haroun stands in front of a golden door.

Haroun GRAND COMPTROLLER OF PROCESSES TOO COMPLICATED TO EXPLAIN. I. M. D. WALRUS, ESQUIRE. KNOCK AND WAIT. (*He knocks.*)

Walrus Come in.

> *The Walrus is not alone.*
>   *In the Walrus's office, grinning broadly, are Prince Bolo, Princess Batcheat, President Mudra of Chup, his aide Miss Blabbermouth, General Kitab, Iff, and Rashid Khalifa, too.*

Haroun Am I in trouble or not?

Everyone except Haroun bursts out laughing.

Walrus You must forgive us. We were pulling your leg. Just our little yolk. Little *yolk*?

All except Haroun laugh again.

Haroun Then what's all this about?

Walrus Haroun Khalifa, to honour you for the incalculable service you have done to the peoples of Kahani and to the Ocean of the Streams of Story, we grant you the right to ask us any favour you desire, and we promise to grant it if we possibly can, even if it means inventing a brand-new Process Too Complicated To Explain.

Rashid Well?

Blabbermouth What is it? What's the matter?

Haroun It's no use asking for anything because what I really want is something nobody here can give me.

Walrus Nonsense, I know perfectly well what you want. You've been on a great adventure, and at the end of great adventures everybody wants the same thing.

Haroun Oh? What's that?

Walrus A happy ending. Happy endings are much rarer in stories, and also in life, than most people think. Because they are so rare, we at P2C2E House have learnt to synthesize them artificially. In plain language: we can make them up.

Haroun That's impossible. They aren't things you can put in bottles.

Walrus If Khattam-Shud could synthesize anti-stories, I should think you'd accept that we can synthesize things, too. As for 'impossible', most people would say that everything that's happened to you lately is quite, quite impossible. Why make a fuss about this particular impossible thing?

Haroun Well. You said it could be a big wish. So it is. I come from a sad city, a city so sad that it has forgotten its name. I want you to provide a happy ending, not just for my adventure, but for the whole sad city as well.

Walrus Happy endings must come at the end of something. If they happen in the middle of a story, or an adventure, all they do is cheer things up for a while.

Haroun That'll do.

Rashid It was time to go home.

Haroun Only now did it occur to Haroun that Rashid must have missed his storytelling appointment in K, and so, no doubt, an angry Snooty Buttoo would be waiting for them.

Enter Butt the Hoopoe.

Hoopoe But but but never mind. When you travel with Butt the Hoopoe, time is on your side. Leave late, arrive early! Let's go! Va-voom-varoom!

Haroun finds Rashid Khalifa sitting on the little balcony at the front of the houseboat, still in his nightshirt, sipping a cup of tea.

Rashid I had such a strange dream . . .

Buttoo Hoo! Halloo!

Haroun Oh Lord, now there will be screaming and shouting and we'll have to pay our own bill.

Buttoo Hoo, somnolent Mr Rashid! Can it be that you and your son are still in your nightshirts, when I am coming to fetch you for the show? Crowds are waiting, tardy Mr Rashid! I trust you will not disappoint.

Haroun This is impossible. (*to Rashid*) Your dream – can you recall it?

Rashid Not now, Haroun. The Shah of Blah is never late.

Chorus Haroun went to get dressed, and noticed a little golden envelope lying by his pillow.

Chorus Inside it was a note written by Blabbermouth and signed by all his friends from the Moon Kahani.

Blabbermouth Come whenever you want.

Iff Stay as long as you like.

Hoopoe Remember when you fly with Butt the Hoopoe, time is on your side.

Chorus There was something else in the golden envelope: a tiny bird, perfect in every detail, cocking its head up at him.

Chorus It was, of course, the Hoopoe.

Rashid You'll recall that Mr Buttoo and his unpopular government were expecting Rashid Khalifa to win them the people's support by telling upbeat praising sagas.

Haroun And a large crowd had indeed gathered to hear Rashid; but from their scowling expressions Haroun gathered that the people didn't care for Mr Buttoo at all.

Buttoo You're on. Much-praised Mr Rashid, you'd better be good, or else.

Rashid Ladies and gentlemen, the name of the tale I am going to tell is 'Haroun and the Sea of Stories'.

Haroun So you didn't forget?

Rashid Did you think I'd forget a story like this one?
   There was once, in the country of Alifbay, a sad city, the saddest of cities, a city so ruinously sad that it had forgotten its name.

Chorus The Gift of the Gab had returned, and Rashid had the audience right in the palm of his hand.

Chorus When he was talking about Khattam-Shud, and his henchmen from the Union of the Zipped Lips, the whole audience stared very hard at Snooty Buttoo and his henchmen, who were sitting behind Rashid on the stage.

Chorus And when Rashid told the audience how almost all the Chupwalas had hated the Cultmaster all along, but had been afraid to say so, well, then a loud murmur of sympathy ran through the crowd.

Chorus And after the fall of the two Khattam-Shuds, somebody started up a chant of: 'Mister Buttoo – go for good. Mister Buttoo – khattam-shud,' and the entire audience joined in.

All Mister Buttoo – go for good!
Mister Buttoo – khattam-shud!

Snooty Buttoo slinks off the stage with his henchmen. The crowd pelt him with rubbish.

Chorus Mr Buttoo was never seen again in the Valley of K, which left the people of K free to choose leaders they actually liked.

The crowd breaks up. Haroun and Rashid are left alone.

Rashid Of course we didn't get paid.

Mr Butt drives up in his bus.

Mr Butt But but but I will escort you home. Best seats have been kept. No problem.

Haroun It was still raining cats and dogs when they returned to the sad city.

Rashid Who cares? Let's walk home. I haven't had a good soaking in years.

Haroun has been worried that Rashid will be depressed about returning to the apartment full of broken clocks and no Soraya. But the wetter he gets, the more boyishly happy he becomes. The streets are full of people fooling around, running and jumping and splashing and falling and, above all, laughing their heads off.

Looks like this old city finally learnt to have fun.

Haroun But why? Nothing's really changed, has it? Look, the sadness factories are still in production.

Rashid We've been out of town, sir. Has something happened while we've been away? A miracle, for example?

Passer-by 1 It's just the rain. It's making everybody happy. Me included. Whee! Whoopee!

Haroun It's the Walrus, making my wish come true. There must be artificial happy endings mixed up with the rain. It's all fake. People should be happy when there's something to be happy about.

Passer-by 2 I'll tell you what to be happy about. We remembered the city's name. It is Kahani. Isn't that a beautiful name for a city? It means 'story', you know.

They turn into their own lane, and see their house.
   Rashid is still hopping and bounding gaily along, but Haroun's feet grow heavier with each step.

Haroun Haroun found his father's cheerfulness simply unbearable, and he blamed the Walrus for it all, for everything fake in the whole wide motherless world.

Oneeta O, too fine, you are returned! What sweets and celebrations we will have!

Haroun What is there to celebrate?

Oneeta To speak personally, I have said good riddance to Mr Sengupta. And I also have a job, in the chocolate factory, and as many chocolates as I require are free of charge. And also I have several admirers – but listen to me, how shameless, talking like this to you!

Haroun I'm happy for you. But in our life it is not all songs and dances.

Oneeta Maybe you have been away too long. Things change.

   The front door of the Khalifa apartment opens, and there stands Soraya Khalifa.

Rashid Is this the Walrus's work too?

Soraya What Walrus? I don't know any Walrus, but I know that I made a mistake. I went; I don't deny. I went, but now, if you want, then I am back.

   Rashid can't speak.

That Sengupta, I swear. What a skinny, scrawny, snivelling, drivelling, mingy, stingy, measly, weaselly clerk! As far as I'm concerned he's finished with, done for, gone for good.

Haroun Khattam-shud.

Soraya That's right. I promise. Mr Sengupta is khattam-shud.

Rashid Welcome home.

The three Khalifas fall into one another's arms. Not wanting to be left out, Miss Oneeta joins them.

Soraya Come inside. There is a limit to how much rain a person can enjoy.

Chorus That night, when he went to bed, Haroun took the miniaturized Butt the Hoopoe out of its little golden envelope and put it on the palm of his left hand.

Haroun Please understand, it's really good to know you'll be here when I need you. But the way things are just now, I honestly don't need to go anywhere at all.

Hoopoe But but but no problem.

Chorus Haroun put Butt the Hoopoe back in its envelope, put the envelope under his pillow, put the pillow under his head and fell asleep.

Chorus When he woke up there were new clothes laid out at the foot of his bed, and on his bedside table was a new clock, fully operational and telling the right time.

Haroun Presents? What's all this?

Chorus Then he remembered: it was his birthday.

Haroun Yes, time is definitely on the move again around these parts.

Chorus Outside, in the living room, his mother had begun to sing.

The End.